How Many Sleeps?

Amber Stewart
and Layn Marlow

OXFORD
UNIVERSITY PRESS

T oast woke one morning and knew that something exciting was going to happen, and it was going to happen soon.

To Justin. Sleep peacefully. A.S.
For the very patient Spencer, Theo and Tegan. L.M.

OXFORD
UNIVERSITY PRESS

Great Clarendon Street, Oxford OX2 6DP

Oxford University Press is a department of the University of Oxford.
It furthers the University's objective of excellence in research, scholarship,
and education by publishing worldwide in

Oxford New York

Auckland Cape Town Dar es Salaam Hong Kong Karachi
Kuala Lumpur Madrid Melbourne Mexico City Nairobi
New Delhi Shanghai Taipei Toronto

With offices in
Argentina Austria Brazil Chile Czech Republic France Greece
Guatemala Hungary Italy Japan Poland Portugal Singapore
South Korea Switzerland Thailand Turkey Ukraine Vietnam

British Library Cataloguing in Publication Data available

ISBN-13: 978-0-19-279188-5 (hardback)
ISBN-10: 0-19-279188-5 (hardback)

ISBN-13: 978-0-19-279189-3 (paperback)
ISBN-10: 0-19-279189-3 (paperback)

10 9 8 7 6 5 4 3 2 1

Printed in China

He could smell it in the quiet morning air, in the mist still hugging the ground, in the autumn leaves trembling on the branches ready to tumble a golden blanket over the wood.

Toast watched, waiting for
the first leaf to fall . . .

… because when the first leaf fell,
that meant it was nearly his birthday.

'How many sleeps till my birthday?'
he asked, as Mummy tucked him in.
'Too many to start counting now,'
smiled Mummy.

'How many sleeps till my birthday?'
Toast asked the next night, and the next, until one
night Mummy said, 'Just enough sleeps to deliver
party invitations to all your friends.'

So the next day that is exactly what they did.
They delivered invitations all the way from Little Hollow …

… to Big Oak Tree,

… to Rabbit, Foxy,

and Squirrel Red Tail.

'How many sleeps till my birthday now, Mummy?'
murmured Toast, so tired from his long walk.
'Just enough sleeps to go collecting decorations,'
whispered Mummy.

After breakfast, they gathered armfuls of gold and rubies, of candles and lanterns.

'How many sleeps till my birthday,
from this exact moment?' Toast wondered,
right in the middle of his bedtime story.
'Exactly enough sleeps to help Mummy
ice the cake,' said Daddy.

In the morning, Mummy iced the cake,
and Toast licked the bowl.

Then together they decorated it so that it was
the best birthday cake Toast had ever seen.

In bed each evening, Toast lay
dreaming of invitation delivering,
of decoration collecting, of
beautiful birthday cakes, and
of what his present might be.

And each evening Mummy wondered, quite loudly,
'Do you think there are enough sleeps until
Toast's birthday?'

'Sleep doesn't come into it!' hrumphed Daddy,
who *had* been dozing in his favourite chair.

'Guess how many sleeps now, Toast?'
said Mummy one morning.

'How many?' wailed Daddy.

'Just enough to pack the party bags, put the candles
on the cake, and get an extra special early night . . .'

'But that means –' squeaked Toast, 'that means –
my birthday is tomorrow!'

And it was.

When Toast's special day had drawn to an end –

when the friends had all come,

the presents loved,

the 'thank yous' given,

the party games played,

and the delicious cake all eaten up –

and Toast was tucked up in bed,

he whispered dreamily,

'How many sleeps till my **next** birthday?'

'Just enough sleeps for Daddy
to start on your next present,'
Mummy whispered back.

But Toast was already asleep.